RapperBee

Poems to give you a buzz...

FORD ST

RAPPERBEE

POEMS TO GIVE YOU A BUZZ...

HARRY LAING

ILLUSTRATIONS BY
ANNE RYAN

FORD ST

To all young readers who want a buzz — HL

More than a word ... for the children — AR

First published by Ford Street Publishing, Melbourne, Victoria, Australia

2 4 6 8 10 9 7 5 3 1

This publication is copyright. Apart from any use as permitted under the Copyright Act 1968, no part may be reproduced by any process without prior written permission from the publisher. Requests and enquiries concerning reproduction should be addressed to Ford Street Publishing Pty Ltd, 162 Hoddle Street, Abbotsford, Vic 3067, Australia

Life of a Dollar Coin and *Trucks* were published in The School Magazine.
Abracadoodling was published in Caterpillar Magazine.

Text copyright © Harry Laing 2021
Illustrations copyright © Anne Ryan 2021

ISBN: 9781925804775 (paperback)

Ford Street website: www.fordstreetpublishing.com
First published 2021

 A catalogue record for this book is available from the National Library of Australia

Design & layout: Marchese Design

Printed in Australia by SOS Print + Media

Contents

Fried Lies	1
RapperBee	2
Mushrooms	4
What Kind of Ologist Are You?	5
Dreams of a School Carpet	6
Wild River (Saved for Ever)	7
Song of a Thumb	8
My Name Is Cheese	10
The Laugh That Escaped	12
Marshmallow Man	13
Glass Lady	14
Pencil Man vs Rubber Man	16
Moon Poem	19
Plastic Is Coming	20
That's Fly-Bizz	22
Haast's Eagle Attacks Moa	24
Life of a Dollar Coin	26
Old Skin	27
The Teacher from the Past	28
The Flattering Sound of Fl	30
A Bee Poem in the Sound of Ee	32
A True Story in the Sound of Oo	34
A Shivery Poem in the Sound of I	36
Clock Shock	37
Bon	38
Monkey Business	40
Step Back Ten Million Years	43
The Lord Howe Island Stick Insect	44
Chicken Rapper	46
Onelineforthewind	48
What Are You Made Of	49
I Wish I Had a Really Scottish Name	50
Ben the Burp	52
Limericks	54

Contents continued

Riddles	55
Chant of the Bunyip Bird	56
Shoctopus, the Underwater Boss	58
See Ya Smoke	60
Crabby Yabbie	62
Sausagepoem	64
The Big Sneeze	65
Regent Honeyeater	66
Bat Talk	68
Abracadoodling	69
MoonFish Chant	70
Cockie-Rap	72
Jimi Hendrix and His Guitar	74
Turbo-Fan	75
The Greatest Heart in History	76
Trucks	78
Giant Kelp	79
Going Back in Time 100 Years to 1920	80
Don't Mention It	81
Take Care in the Top End	82
The Wave You've Waited For	84
Yawn Alert	85
My Favourite Food	86
Wa, the Crow	87
I Wanna Be a Wombat	88
Chair Rodeo	90
The Strangest Pet	91
The Adventures of a Foot	92
Nightmare of the Nose	94
Big Black Bulls	96
Storm at Night	98
Stingrays	99
When You Feel Sad Sing This Song	100

Fried Lies

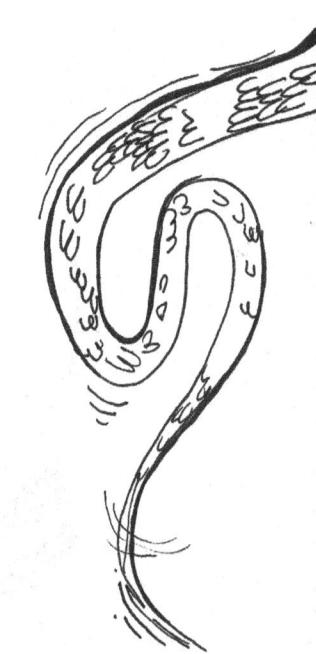

For breakfast I eat wildebeest
my lunch is fried piranha
dinner is a carpet snake
topped with mashed banana

my sister is an aeroplane
Mum lives on the roof
Dad loves his pet pistachio
he's nuts and that's the truth

five times five is forty two
I've never had a shower
I've been to Mars, it's not that far
it took me half an hour

my other name is SuperFly,
my favourite sport is sleeping
I think I am a car alarm
when you bump me I start beeping

so if you're going to tell a lie
make sure it's big and shiny
otherwise your brain will fry
and your poem will be tiny.

Rapper Bee

zub zub zub zz zz
zub zub zub zz zz
zub zub zub zz zz zz zz

zo, I am the RapperBee
you gonna rap with me?
I'm the power to the flowers
I'm the livin of the buzz
I'm the neatest I'm the sweetest
RapperBee that ever was

I've got rhythm I've got timin'
and my brilliance is blindin'
I do words instead of honey
I'm the buzz I am the money

I'm the push in the bush
and the zoom in the bloom
pack a sting with ma bling
you can see through ma wings

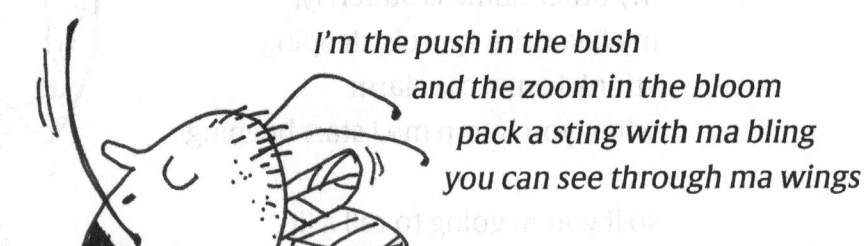

cos I'm the RapperBee
and you can flatter me
I'm faster than the flies
and I'm speedin' through the skies
I am the RapperBee
why don't you rap with me

*I'm the fur and the fuzz
and the bloom in the buzz
I'm the zip in the sip
and the swarm in the storm
cos I'm always performin'
ma rhythm is freein'
and rap is ma being*

zub zub zub zz zz
zub zub zub zz zz
zub zub zub zz zz
RapperBeeeeeeeeeeeeeeeeeeeeeeeeeee

Mushrooms

ring of ivory buttons
overnight apparitions
shiny with dew
each
one
brand
new

little white fists
punched through grass
something has nibbled
them
on the
way
past

pick a new mushroom
brush off dirt-crumbs
slice into the pan
fry with
butter
and yum!

What Kind of Ologist Are You?

When you're a dogologist
you study dogs

    Frogologists tend to get
    married to frogs

logologists love
to roll on the ground

    bogologists look into bogs
    (they can drown!)

a jogologist's job
is to run out of breath

    a shockologist's dream
    is to scare you to death

a megalollyholidayologist
is probably the best.

Dreams of a School Carpet

I am the lowest of the low
there is no lower you could go

just look at me, I'm flat-out bored
trampled, battered, and ignored

but in my dreams I lift and fly
a carpet-eagle in the sky

or I go gliding through the sea
flapping my wings like a Manta Ray . . .

OK . . . it's just a dream, I'm stuck
and you're all piled up on my back

I'm hanging out for half past three
when the cleaners come to me

and vacuum my poor old face
it's like a massage, it's so nice . . .

and then I'm left alone to dream –
before you lot come screaming in.

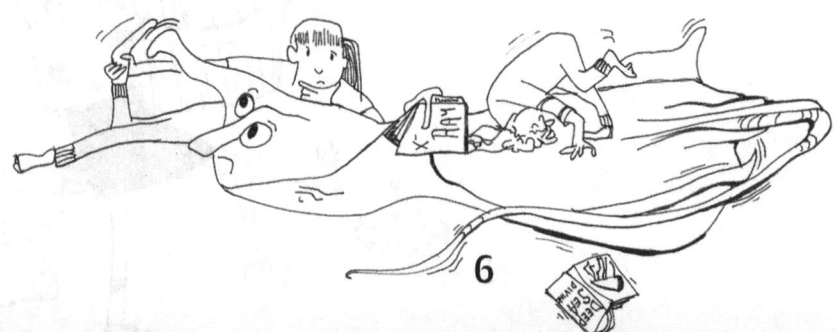

Wild River (Saved For Ever)

Caramel swirls
        as the river runs free
white-petal curls
        in pools of black tea
a drift of gold leaves
        from the Sassafras tree

rocks edged like blades
        in deep myrtle shade
white-knuckle falls
        and dripping moss walls
heart-racing churns
        where ice-water burns
giant fallen trees
        like vast ribs and knees

cliffs tower over
        old as Gondwana
this wild-running river
        untamed for ever

Song of a Thumb

Thumb thumb thumb
I'm not dumb
I'm hopping down the street

my hand is gone
and I'm alone
I'm growing tiny feet

thumb thumb thumb
I live on crumbs
a matchbox is my bed

thumb thumb thumb
I'm scared of shoes
be careful where you tread

I've learnt to swim
and climb a tree
I don't need a family

I'm going to try
and find a bird
to teach me how to fly

thumb thumb thumb
I'm on the run
don't ask the reason why.

My Name Is Cheese

I'm strong I'm chill and chunky
and I'm flavoursome and funky
more bouncy than a monkey
I'm a champion, I'm cheese!

I am bendy you can squeeze me
when you grill me you just thrill me
try and grate me you won't kill me
I'm resilient, I'm cheese!

keep your chocolate and chorizo
chewy chicken, stinky peas
I'm the guy with all the flavour
  I'm the biggest block of cheese

  I will bubble on your pizza
    I'm more bitey than your teacher
      from my head down to my knees
        every bit of me is cheese

so let's hear my name again

      cheese!

and who would you like to meet?

      cheese!

and whaddya want to eat?

      cheese!

who's gonna save the world?

      cheese!

yes cheese!

The Laugh That Escaped

There was a silent laugh
shaking and quaking
inside a person
silently
but the laugh wanted to hear itself
so that crafty laugh
    broke the person in half ... *ha!*
    ha ha ha ha ha!
    the laugh was out
    the laugh was free
    laughed at buses stuck in trees
laughed at icy-poles and bees
laughed at every kind of stuff
ha ha ha ha!
it realised it couldn't stop
was out of puff and longed to drop
that crafty laugh had had enough
it rasped and gasped *ha ha*
and choked and croaked *ha*
was forced to crawl back inside its owner
and soon the both of them
shook happily again with silent laughter.

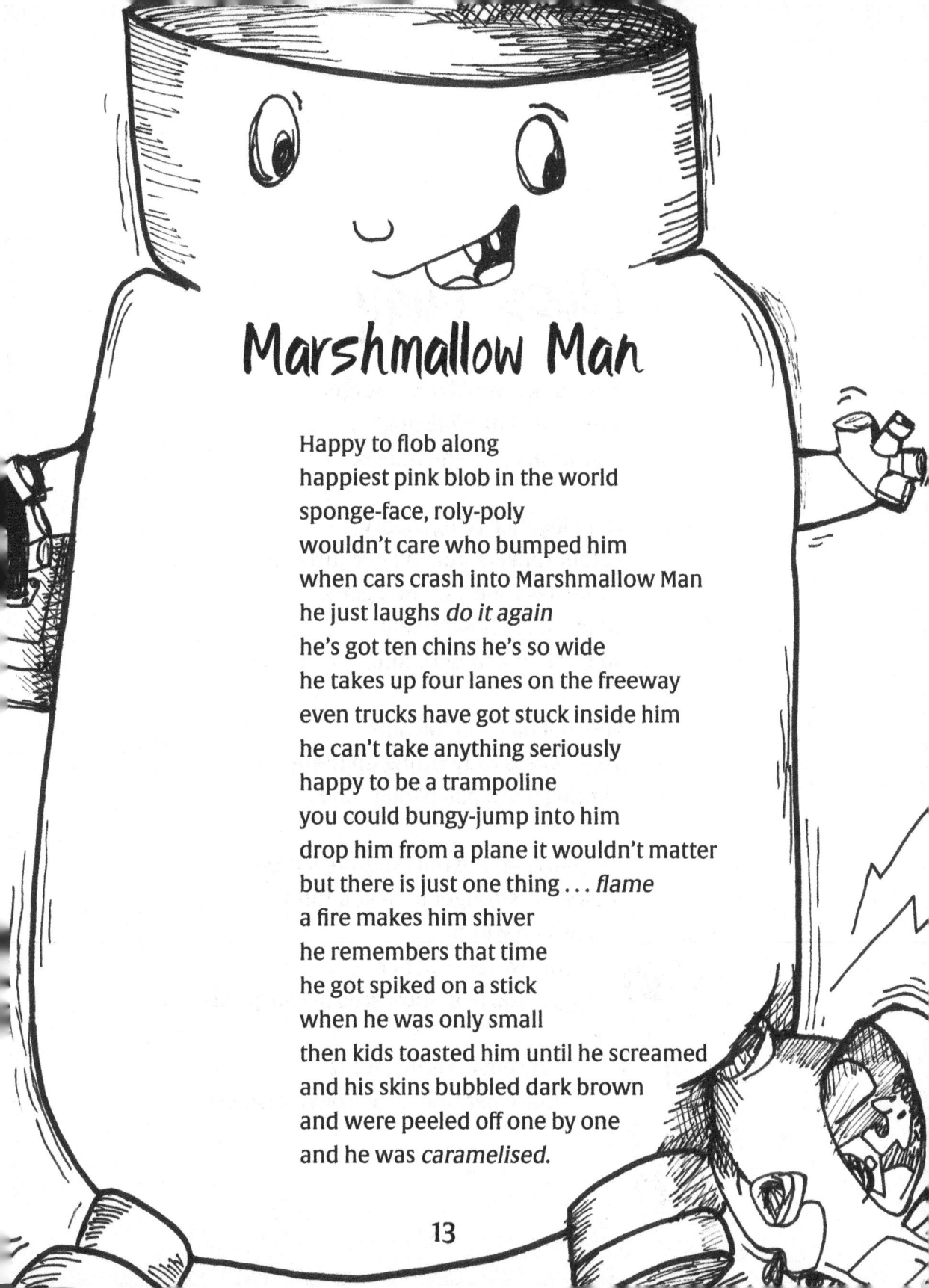

Marshmallow Man

Happy to flob along
happiest pink blob in the world
sponge-face, roly-poly
wouldn't care who bumped him
when cars crash into Marshmallow Man
he just laughs *do it again*
he's got ten chins he's so wide
he takes up four lanes on the freeway
even trucks have got stuck inside him
he can't take anything seriously
happy to be a trampoline
you could bungy-jump into him
drop him from a plane it wouldn't matter
but there is just one thing... *flame*
a fire makes him shiver
he remembers that time
he got spiked on a stick
when he was only small
then kids toasted him until he screamed
and his skins bubbled dark brown
and were peeled off one by one
and he was *caramelised*.

Glass Lady

has a voice you'll never forget
a distant *clink clink* tinkling
and winking as she moves.

Her elegance is legendary
colour reflects from all her surfaces
some days she's stained glass
others days crystal clear
so bright you need sunnies to see her.

See that flash on the hill?
That's Glass Lady sitting up there
glinting like a pile of diamonds –

I suppose you're thinking she'll break
well she's stronger than you think
    she's no wimp
        throw rocks at her
            you'll be showered in sharp glass darts.

        My advice is just wave
    admire her brilliance from a distance.

Pencil Man vs Rubber Man

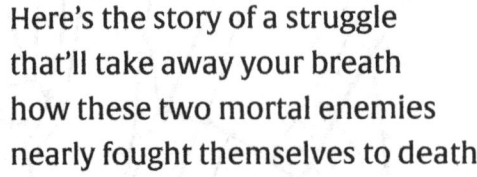

Here's the story of a struggle
that'll take away your breath
how these two mortal enemies
nearly fought themselves to death

Pencil Man is slimline smart
he's quick, he's on the ball
but Rubber Man's the bendy best
and ultra-flexible

Pencil Man is on his feet
sharpened up real good
he can draw as fast as anyone
he's a lethal piece of wood

Rubber Man is yawning
he's cunning and he's mean
there's nothing that he can't erase
he'll rub the whole world clean

so everyone is waiting
who is gonna win
will Pencil Man come out on top
or this be the end of him?

Rubber Man is grinning
Pencil Man begins to write
Rubber Man wipes every word
this is going to be a fight

Pencil Man draws lightning
Rubber Man gets struck
Pencil Man draws Rubber Man
inside a garbage truck

Rubber Man backflips and kicks
cracks Pencil Man down low
Pencil Man has lost some lead
he's drawing way too slow

Pencil Man is limping
Rubber Man has worn too thin
he shouts at Pencil Man
you're gonna end up in the bin!

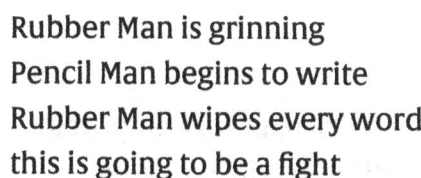
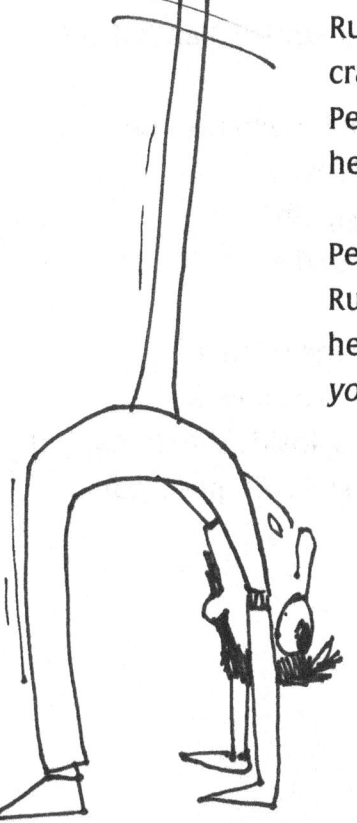

Pencil Man is getting weak
his line is just a scrawl
there's really nothing left of him
he's centimetres tall

but Rubber Man's a sliver
rubbed to his last shreds
when Pencil Man has one last go
he writes *Rubber Man is dead*

and Rubber Man has got no strength
to rub those words away
falls into the rubbish bin
that's a dirty way to die

so Pencil Man's the winner
let's give him all a cheer . . .
No! He's stuck inside the sharpener!
Pencil Man has disappeared!

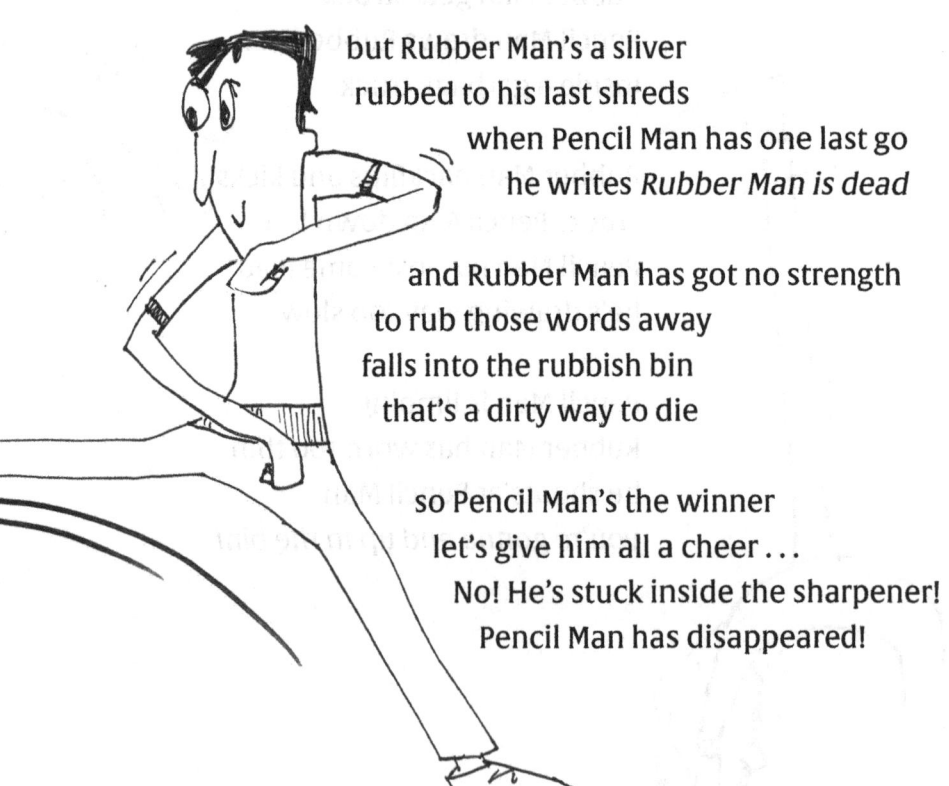

Moon Poem

hey
look
low in
the sky
outline
of silver
that disc
whittled
to a sliv-
er I love
how the
new moon
catches my
eye it gives
me a tin-
gle a shiver
greeting
her crisp
shape sud-
denly in
place telling
m e s o m e -
thing good
is about to
happen

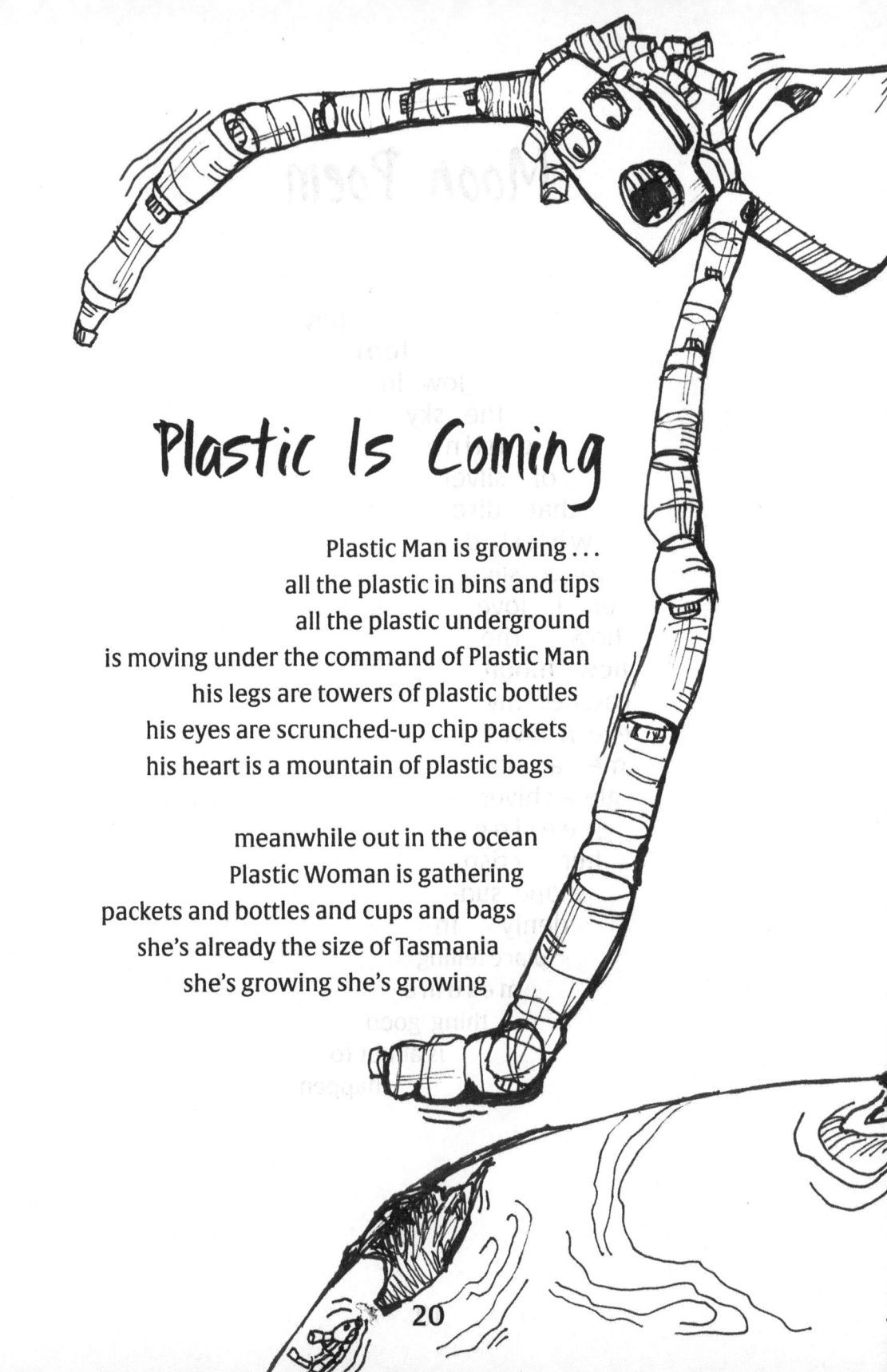

Plastic Is Coming

Plastic Man is growing . . .
all the plastic in bins and tips
all the plastic underground
is moving under the command of Plastic Man
his legs are towers of plastic bottles
his eyes are scrunched-up chip packets
his heart is a mountain of plastic bags

meanwhile out in the ocean
Plastic Woman is gathering
packets and bottles and cups and bags
she's already the size of Tasmania
she's growing she's growing

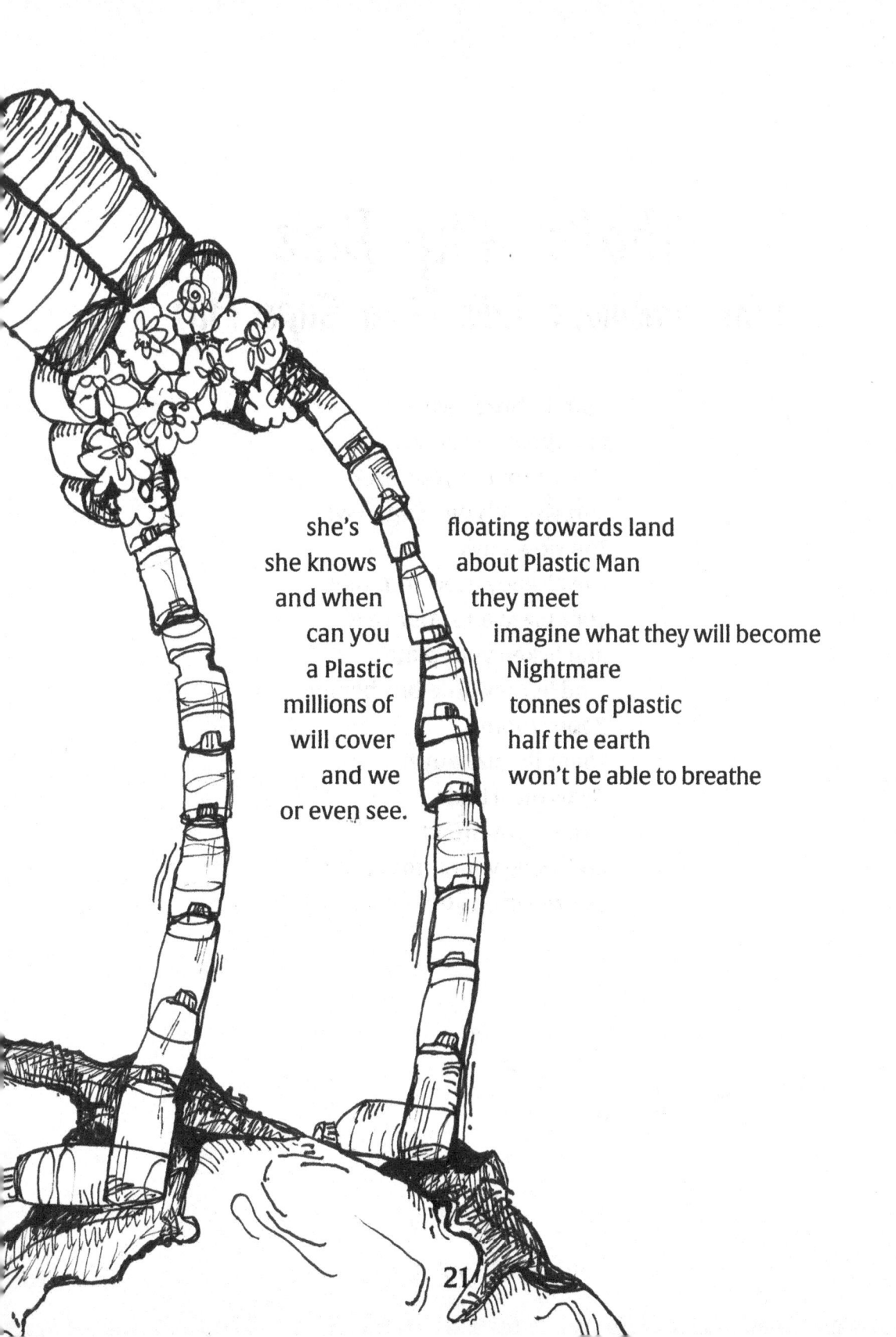

she's floating towards land
she knows about Plastic Man
and when they meet
can you imagine what they will become
a Plastic Nightmare
millions of tonnes of plastic
will cover half the earth
and we won't be able to breathe
or even see.

That's Fly-Bizz
(The Fabulous Life of a SuperFly)

Born to buzz I was
and drive you crazy.
What's that in your eye?
Surprise! It's me, SuperFly!
Too slow guys
I've already tried your pies
your pizza and your cake
and licked your plate
(and left my little bits behind . . .)
Zoom zoom!
That's fly-bizz guys!
Gives me a buzz
to hear you shout
and wave your arms about
as I whizz up your nose.

You'd love to flick me
swat me squash me
sorry I'm too busy
sipping from your tea.
It's me again
bouncing off the windows
just to make you dizzy.
Woah, you are so slow!
and I'm the pro.
When will you realise
that's fly-bizz, guys?
Zoom zoom!

Haast's Eagle Attacks Moa

Eagle circling
sky darkening
danger growing

    Moa sensing
    fear clenching
    muscle tensing

Eagle turning
eye burning
wings folding

    Moa running
    legs churning
    breath rasping

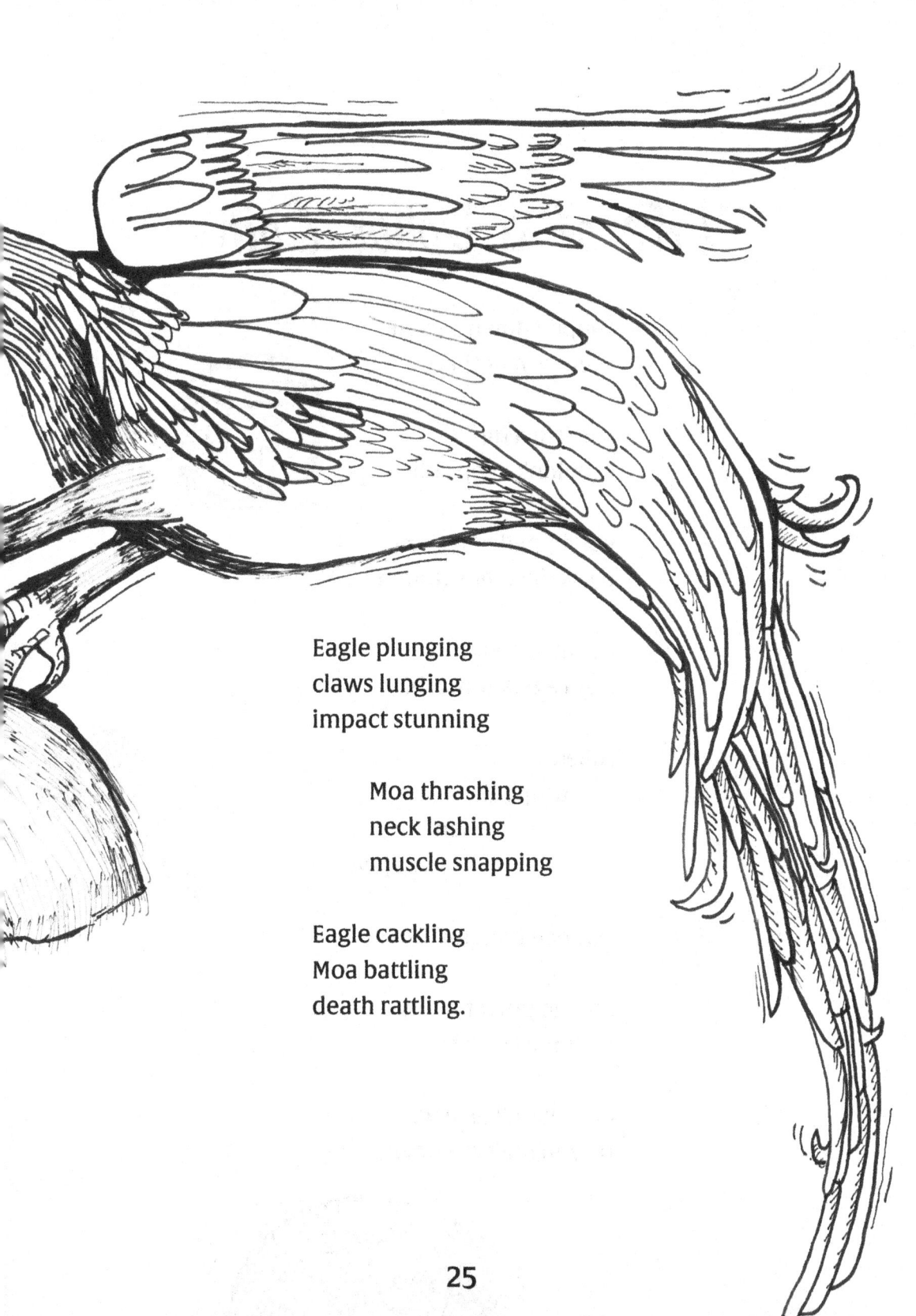

Eagle plunging
claws lunging
impact stunning

Moa thrashing
neck lashing
muscle snapping

Eagle cackling
Moa battling
death rattling.

Life of a Dollar Coin

Slipped down a chair
spent a year there

stuck in a till
I couldn't keep still

got flipped and spun
by a cricketer's thumb

ran in a stream
from a poker machine

rolled
    dropped
        stolen
            swopped

scraped bent lost spent

I'm the power of one
your pocket sun

and I won't give up
till you melt me down.

Old Skin

Ever seen a snake skin?
The empty shell of a spider?
Have you handled
the husk of a cicada?
What if your skin starts to itch
like it's too tight
and there's a tingling in your toes
which spreads to your knees
your hands chest head
now the tingling is behind your eyes
you're flexing stretching
twisting tearing and running
to a place no one can see you
and guess what
you unzip yourself
step out of your old skin
and you look down
and there it is lying on the ground
crumpled like a onesie.

The Teacher from the Past

Good afternoon, you lovely class
I'm your new teacher... from the past.

The past where things were not the same
we had discipline back then: no games.

Here are the rules that you will follow
no one moves and no one swallows.

Who made that noise? – you, stand up straight.
Stay behind till very late.

Does someone want to blow their nose?
they can wait till they explode.

Your first test: six times six . . .
WRONG! Go outside and pick up bricks.

People sometimes say I'm mean
but are you sure your ears are clean?

Once a year I can be jolly
who'd like to try this vintage lolly?

it's mint with a spider-flavoured centre
crunchy, tangy, you won't find better.

Aren't you glad that I am here
I'm your new teacher for this year.

The Flattering Sound of Fl

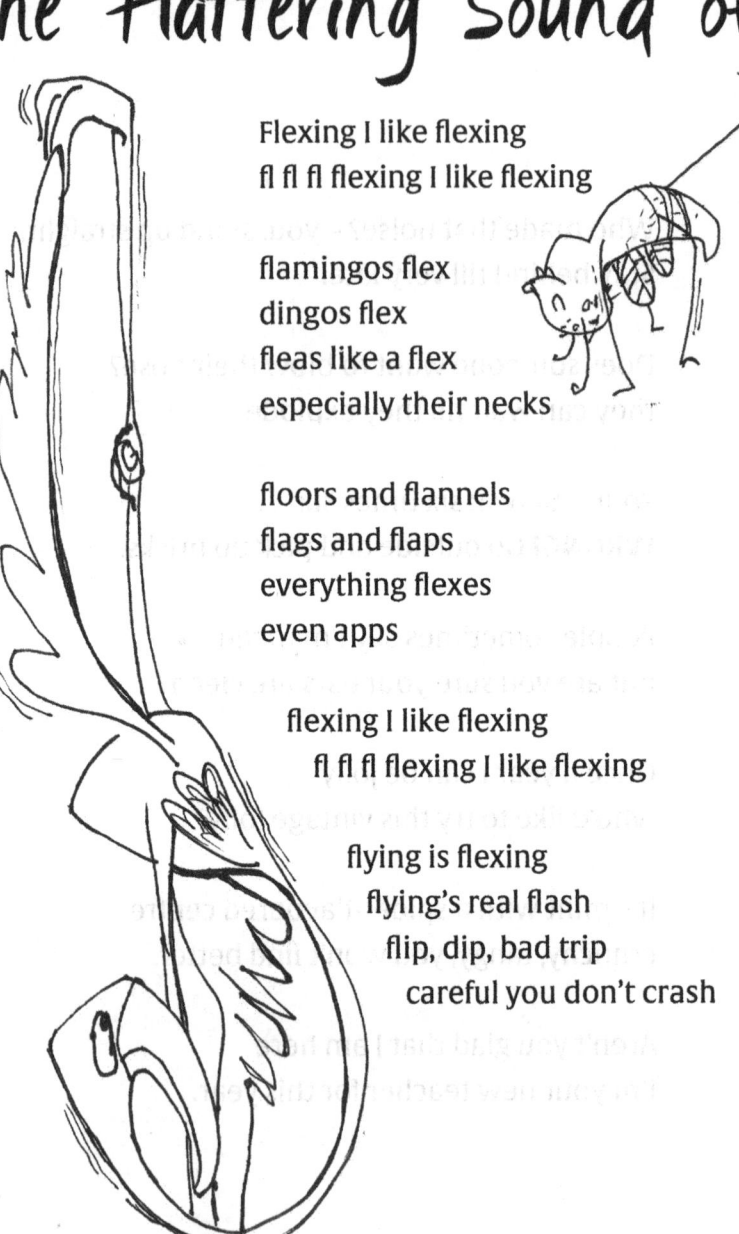

Flexing I like flexing
fl fl fl flexing I like flexing

flamingos flex
dingos flex
fleas like a flex
especially their necks

floors and flannels
flags and flaps
everything flexes
even apps

flexing I like flexing
fl fl fl flexing I like flexing

flying is flexing
flying's real flash
flip, dip, bad trip
careful you don't crash

flexing I like flexing
fl fl fl flexing I like flexing

flowers are flexible
flies are too
flex when you're flossing
and your teeth are like new

flea flap flannel rap
flick it to the floor
flexing like a flip flop
flocking out the door

A Bee Poem in the Sound of Ee

eee eee
it's me, freaky bee
teeny machine seeking honey
feeling trees with my antennae

eee eee
I'm a freaky bee with fleas
that squeeze and tease me
sneaky sleazy fleas
it's not easy keeping clean
being a bee
because of the honey

luckily
bees are a team
keen never dreamy
streaming into the trees
even in breezes

heee heee

A True Story in the Sound of Oo

Once in a blue moon . . . spooky!
your shoes and boots lose it
zoom out of your room
into the moonlight
to cruise around and hoon.

Who's on the news?
your boots and shoes

A Shivery Poem in the Sound of I

Drip drip . . .
an evil mist
fills the city

things with twisted fingers
slither and hiss

is this fiction? I wish . . .
my limbs are fixed

my skin chills
this thing tickles my wrist
grips
lifts its pincers . . .
quick
the silver stick
flick the insect
flick the switch

invisible is bliss.

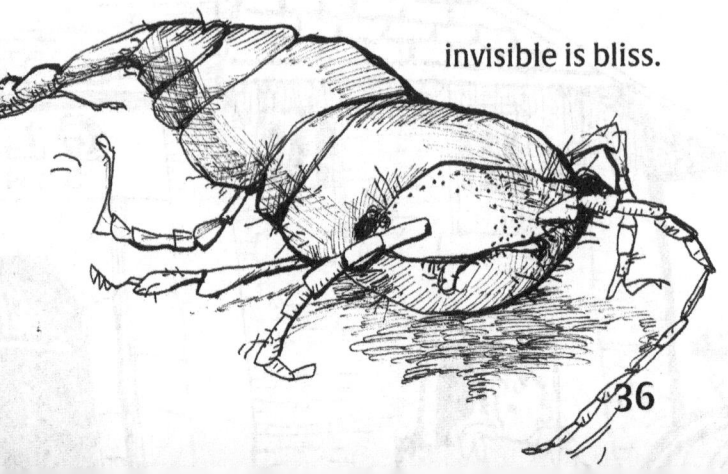

Clock Shock

I am a slave
I work for time
the way I'm treated
is a crime

don't slow down
is what they say
I never get
a holiday

I'd love to lose
my hands, my face
and travel to
a timeless place

no more seconds
no more hours
no more minutes –

I'd count the flowers.

Bon

Bon's a twist
he's a loop
corners fast
he's a scoop

he scampers, he bounces
he whimpers, he pounces,

and he chews and he chews and he chews
he loves cardboard
and plastic and wood
he's so good

now he's eating my laces
and licking my face, yes

then he sleeps
for an hour
        before waking and stretching
              he's back to full power

he's skidding and kidding
and sliding and gliding
and running and spinning
and tumbling and fumbling

everything's fun for him
he's just a puppy called Bon
and he's full on.

Monkey Business

This monkey's from another dimension
he just loves your total attention
uses his fur to soak it up
he can't get enough so please don't stop

      monkey's got a whole lot of bend
      monkey is my very special friend
      he doesn't care about gravity
      treats everyone like they're a tree

monkey's got a fabulous feature
uses his tail to hook on a teacher
teacher doesn't know the simple fact
they've got a monkey hanging on their back

    monkey's got a whole lot of bend
    monkey is my very special friend
    he doesn't care about gravity
    treats everyone like they're a tree.

Step Back Ten Million Years

Before schools
before rules
before Google
before noodles
before fridges
and bridges
trains drains
socks laptops
nails sails
cars jars
mugs drugs
shoes news
before tins bins
pans vans
cities jetties
toys noise
before noise noise

NOISE

step back ten million years
it's so quiet
all you can hear
is a giant wombat
chewing.

The Lord Howe Island Stick Insect

I'm a giant stick insect, glossy and brave
I live on Lord Howe above the waves,
I'm the rarest insect in the world
and here's my story: it needs to be told.

Back in 1918 a ship was wrecked
hundreds of black rats ran unchecked
gobbled my ancestors, that's how it was.
People thought I was gone but I wasn't because

in 2001 a team came my way
climbed Ball's Pyramid to look for me
and surprise, surprise, under just one bush
twenty four of us clustered, we were in no rush.

Two pairs of me were sent to the zoo
and you won't believe it but this is true
we bred so well we're more than ten thousand
and we're ready to go back to Lord Howe Island

but first they've had to remove the rats
and here's the news: they've almost done that!
The island will soon be safe for me
I'll be munching on my melaleuca tree.

I'm a giant stick insect – I'm tough, I'm strong
soon I'll be back where I belong
and I'll be a legend because I hung on
yes I'll be a legend because I hung on.

Chicken Rapper

I met this chicken on the road
have you ever met a chicken about to explode?

he was peckin' he was frettin'
he was flappin' his wings
he was doin' those crazy chicken things

and he stamps the ground
and he goes bright red
tryin to find the right words in his head

buck buck buck buck buck buckie
buck buck buck buck buck buckie

I said chicken bird give me a word
I said chicken bird c'mon give me a word

he said egg I said leg
he said look I said cook
he said toast I said roast
he said fried? I said hide!

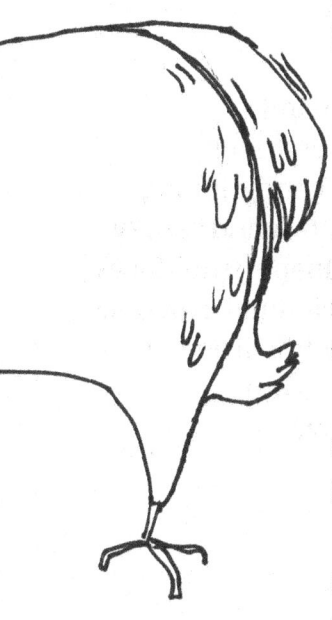

he was runnin' he was flappin'
he was losin his head
   cos he was getting worried
   I was rhymin' him dead

  aw, c'mon chicken no need to run
you and me we can have some fun
we got time and it's no crime
we can bust some crazy rhymes

and he said *buck buck buck buck buck buckie*
I said *truck truck truck truckie truckie*

that chicken bird he lay down on the road
next thing I saw the chicken explode.

Onelineforthewind

Windwitcherywaywardwindwhat'sinthewind
whenit'swindingupwantingandwillingeverything
bendsinthebigwindthingsholdongrabbingandgripping
asthewindscrabblesandsquabblesseemsthiswind'sangry
thewayitsnatchespeoplesbreathandsandpaperstheirfaces-
sothey'vegoneallblotchyandredandthiswindmakespeople
grumpylookattheirhairallovertheplaceandthelittledog
withbigearsflappingwheeliebinsrollingdownthe
streetthissswindreallyiissphhhhhfwwwww
ccchhhhhhhgottafindsomewhoooo
ooossssshhshelter
outofthiswind

What Are You Made Of

Here's the answer
you're a star
hydrogen oxygen carbon water
you're made of atoms
and atoms don't die
they live for ever
so get this
you're stardust
you were born in an explosion
before space existed
before schools existed
billions of years ago something went
BOOM!
you are the ripple of that sound
you are the dust of the explosion
you are breathing in bits of Captain Cook
you have dinosaur in your brain

so what does it feel like
being around
for ever?

(almost)

I Wish I Had a Really Scottish Name

Who's been to Scotland, och aye!
everyone should go – here's why:

Scottish surnames are the best
McMiles McBetter than the rest

McSporran, McLuggage
McHaggis, McPorridge

McMickmuck, McMonkey
McTwist and McFunky

McHiccup, McNessie
McThistle, McJesse

McSpamwe, McTartan
McGiggle, McFartin

McFishface, McHeather
McHorribleweather

McWhisky, McWobble
McScottie, McDoggle

McOhNo, McNoonoo
McDeep and McDoodoo

McLochloch, McDroppit
McMcMcMcMcMcMcMc

Stoppit!

Ben the Burp

There was a boy
he was a twerp
instead of saying hi
he burped

other people snort
or slurp
Ben would smile
and then he'd burp

Ben the Burp
Ben the Burp
so rude so crude
he wouldn't sturp

until a teacher
hatched a plan
but not in fact
the full burp-ban

this teacher
was a clever man
he said to Ben
burp all you can . . . go on

and Ben began . . .
burped as hard as he could go
burped them fast
burped them slow

until his lungs
went bang and then
one last tiny burp . . . o
no Ben!

Limericks

There was an Old Lady who said
I'm so tired of lying in bed
she found a small rat
put it under her hat
and the rat's made its nest on her head.

I once met a venomous snake
and made this quite simple mistake
I said can you *hisss*
and the snake said *like thisssssss?*
then he bit me and gave me the shakes.

I once met a cranky old man
who was trying to open a can
he was using a spanner
then he picked up a hammer
that cranky old man BAM BAM BAM!

Riddles

I'm not just an empty space
tell you what, I like your face.

Strong and shiny, five and five
don't call me dead cos I'm alive.

I've got a neck but no head
arms but no legs.

Two makes one
I grip your thumb
can't wait to eat
another sheet.

mirror fingernail jumper scissors

Chant of the Bunyip Bird

Ooom ooom
           doof doof
shiver shiver
           shiver shiver
shiver shiver
           shiver shiver

    boom!

from the swamp
           in the night
spooky sound
           out of sight
it's a cow
           it's a frog
like the howl
           of a dog

shaky ground
          all around
coming near
          feel the fear
of a beak
          of a claw
but it stops
          on the shore
and the voice
          fades away
listen up
          what's it say?
it's an ooom
          it's a doof
it's a shiver shiver
          shiver shiver
shiver shiver
          shiver shiver

        boom!

Shoctopus, the Underwater Boss

From my underwater house
  I'm watching you and I'm the boss

  I've got the arms I've got the brain
you think I'm soft well think again

   I practise deep sea martial arts
     I hypnotise with sudden darts

  the way I move is like a spell
    I'm there I'm gone I'm jet-propelled

    tentacular spectacular
      I suit myself by shifting colour

    juicy reds to freezing blues
    orange coral seaweed hues

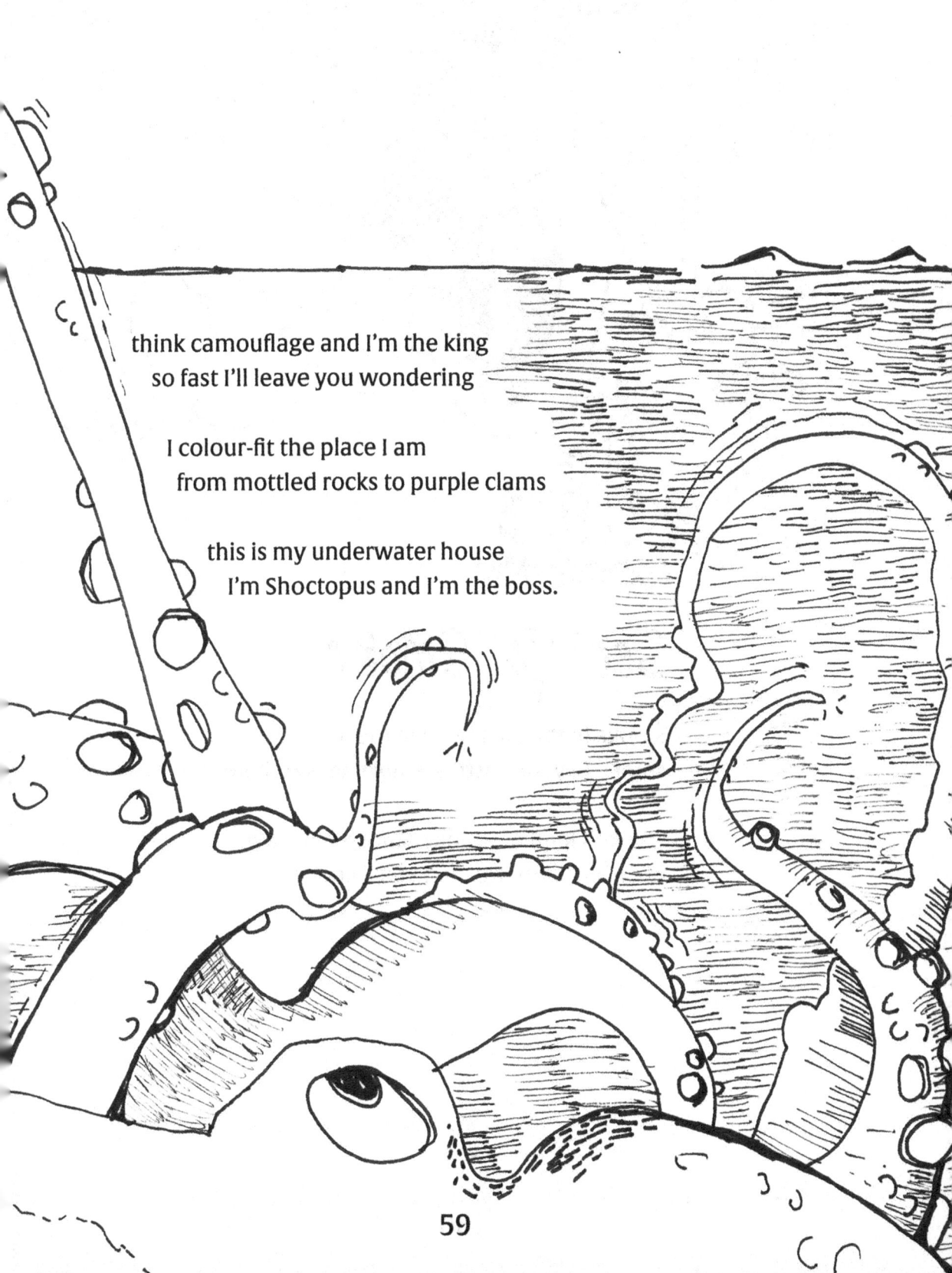

See Ya Smoke

Smoke in the air smoke in the air
smoke in your nostrils, smoke everywhere

smoke's kind of spooky, smoke is no joke
breathing it in, worried you'll choke

sneaky old smoke it sure gets around
sometimes so thick you can't see the ground

but I've invented this brilliant machine
that will suck up the smoke and make the air clean

two kilometres wide and one metre high
it's like a giant mouth and it swims through the sky

and the smoke that it swallows turns into rain
which drops on the fires so they don't start again.

Smoke in the air smoke in the air
smoke in your nostrils, smoke everywhere.

Crabby Yabbie

Down in the Tarkine (that's in Tassie)
I stumbled on a giant yabbie

I was trying to cross a creek
I needed help 'cos it was deep

at first I thought he was a rock
then I got a nasty shock

I've seen plenty rocks before
but none that lift . . . a massive claw!

he watched me with his beady eyes
as I tried to apologise

I poked him with a stick – he snapped it
I threw a river-stone, he cracked it

then I jumped – he grabbed my arm
like he was going to crunch through bone

tore my coat and ripped my shirt
luckily it didn't hurt

I had to break his iron grip
I pivoted, I spun, I flipped

and landed on the other side
   of him – that yabbie was a metre wide

            and then I ran, no going back
             I'm not that yabbie's lunchtime snack!

Sausagepoem

This is a sausage poem
this poem is a sausage
a sizzling Saturday sausage poem
smelling so delicious
look at the sausage smoke drifting
from every word in this poem
driving you mad with hunger
crisp and delicious sausage words
the sausage smoke drifting
are you hungry are you?
do you want to fry more of this poem?
this sizzling sausage poem
will you go crazy waiting?
how many sausage-poems
are lined up on the BBQ of this page?
quick find some sauce words and squeeze them
over your hot sausage poem
wrap them in bread the butter melting
bite, taste, chew, yum and

write another.

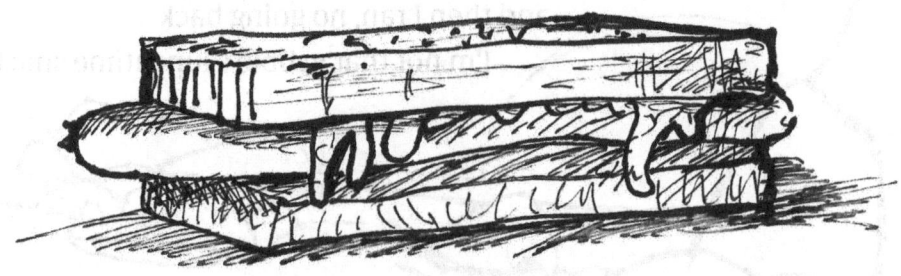

The Big Sneeze

Some days
I just wanna *ahh . . . ahh sneeze*

pollen from trees makes me *sneeze*
if I give my arm a squeeze *sneeze*

the more I try not to *ahh . . . ahh . . . sneeze*
cheese makes me *sneeze*
knees make me *sneeze*

    sometimes it happens
        sneeze times a day
           driving on the *sneeze*   free *sneeze* way

one day   I think   my nose
    will *sneeze*   away

please *sneeze* stop me   *sneeze*
                                       ing

Regent Honeyeater

Black-headed jewel
 with the yellow-edged wings
 where did you come from?
Did you just fly in?

Everyone's watching
 as you bob your head,
  clap your bill, bow
like you know you're the one
you're a spark of the sun.

Yellow-black flash
 fine white lace on your back
  and a band on your leg which we check –
Yes! you're captive-bred

now free in the trees
calling out, just messing about
and we're happy to see you
and count you and look there's no doubt
your numbers are growing

and so are the trees that we've planted
Ironbarks and Spotted Gum
soon they'll have flowers
you get the nectar, we hear your song–

so keep coming, keep reminding us all
you're a jewel in the crown
a Regent, a yellow-black flash of the sun.

Bat Talk

When the sun's almost gone
and the kookas are laughing
that's when I wake
on the wall of my cave
and I shiver and stretch
and head into the dusk.

Night is my friend
seeing by sound
I'm radar on wings
twisting and turning
hunting and feasting.

You wouldn't believe
all the creatures I eat
until light in the east
means the dawn's on its way
and it's time to head back to my cave.

Just don't come looking
you'll hate what you see
I am ugly so ugly
a genius by night –
a freak in the day.

Abracadoodling

When's a woodle not a poodle?
Woodles woo and poodles bark
when a woodle eats a foodle
he leaves a doodle in the park

have you ever tried to google
found a shoogle by mistake?
Or during recess at your scoogle
eaten snoogle in a cake?

Once I schmoozled with a foozle
he called me by my yoozle name
something that you do not doozle
but foozles never take the blame

my advice is: check your stoodle
in case you're moodled by a sheep
otherwise you're in big poodle
yoodle-doodling's never cheap.

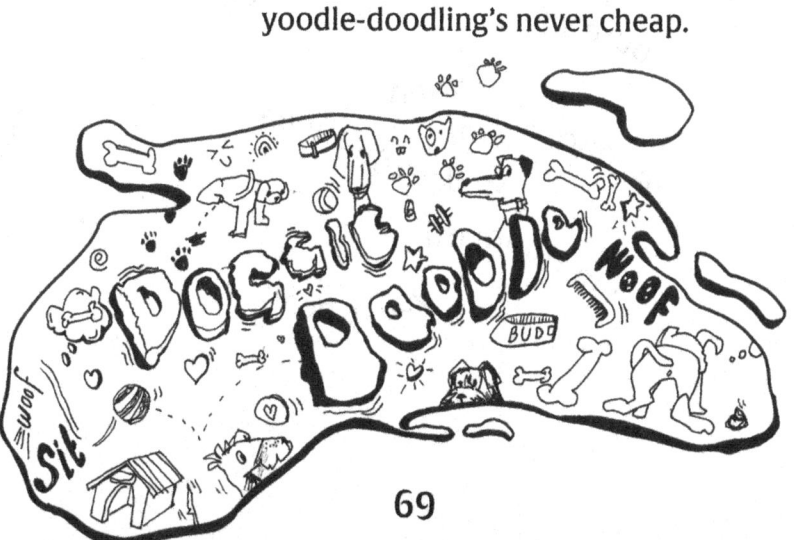

MoonFish Chant

MoonFish is who?
MoonFish is you!
MoonFish is who?
MoonFish is you!
Just passing by
will you stay will you stay?
in the night sky
tell me why tell me why?
I've wishes to grant
and we chant and we chant
I'm pure silver
deliver!
pure silver
deliver!
just once a year
don't disappear
I'm MoonFish
you're here!

Cockie-Rap

Cockie in the cage
with the big dark eye
looks at me carefully
is he a little shy?

hello cockie
   hello cockie
hello cockie
   hello cockie

with his smart white feathers
and a punk yellow crest
he *is* a clever cockie,
and I am so impressed
until he says

go to work
go to school
what's your name
that's so cool

swaying on his perch yeah
grabbin' on the bars
screaming like a crazy bird
who thinks he is a star

go to work
go to school
what's your name
that's so cool

listen cockie
    listen cockie
listen cockie
    listen cockie

then he bows flaps his wings
does the crazy cockie spin
clacks his beak clicks his tongue
cockie's really having fun

go to work
go to school
go and jump
in the pool.

Jimi Hendrix and His Guitar

Jimi
  was the
    best ever.
      This is his 1968
        Gibson Flying V and
          made sounds never heard before, riffs, wails and purple screams. Jimi
            He was a one-man revolution, played guitar upside down, tore sound
              open with his teeth. Hendrix
                was a genius, he
                  was way ahead
                    when he
                      died.

74

Turbo-Fan

I've bust my blades to keep you cool
now it's time to break the rules

today's the day I'm spinning free
no more whispering from me

I start as usual, setting one
give no sign of what's to come

then spin it quickly up to four
vibrations in the walls and floor

books are blowing, this is fun
my revs increase to way past ten

chairs are flying, hair is crazy
the air is full of dust and hazy

I'm screaming like a runway jet
it's as noisy as it gets

turn that fan off teachers cry
as finally I blast my way
through the ceiling, what a day!

The Greatest Heart in History

Yes that's me
I'm Phar Lap's heart

*and I never give up
never give up*

my motive is winning
I keep his blood spinning

I'm the motor the power
I pump and deliver

    and I never give up
    never give up

hear the crowd cheering
I keep the hooves going

    and I never give up
    never give up
    no I never give up

not till the end
and not even then

big from the start
I'm Phar Lap's heart

    and I never give up
    never give up
    no I never give up.

Trucks

Road-snorters
juggernauters

metal-musclers
highway-hustlers

diesel-swallowers
freeway-followers

trucks and trucks and trucks and trucks

hay-wagons
night-dragons

eighty-tonner-
distance-runners

bodies gleaming
gears screaming

rumble-making
footpath-shaking

trucks are shiny trucks are tough
trucks deliver loads of STUFF.

Giant Kelp

swaying arching bending clasping twisting drifting

hustling glistening listening

reaching muscling heaving

furling curling dancing glancing growing slowing

rock-clinging, sea-forest swinging crayfish-sheltering

cold-water kissing, if kelp goes

what would we be missing?

Going Back in Time 100 Years to 1920

I'm walking up a road
in these strange old-fashioned clothes
when I bump into a swagman
with his billy and his pipe
and he asks me the year
I say *2020 mate*
and he puts down his swag
has a scratch and he says
*mate it's either 1920
or I'm a hundred years late*
 and before I can think
  he's got sticks, made a fire
   fried some bread, lit his pipe
    and his hat is a wreck
     his pants one big patch
      but he doesn't seem to care
   and the smell of the fire
    and his pipe and the bread
     makes the day feel so good
      that it must be 1920 and he says
       *I go where I want
         because nobody owns me
          it's good to be free
           are you coming my way?*

Don't Mention It

what is a black hole
  is it round like a doughnut is it soft or hard
does time go backwards in a black   hole
  what if you fell in a black hole
would you come out the other side
  as a toaster or a chicken what if you
started writing and your words
                started
                    falling
                      into
                        a black
                          hole

is this page is a black hole
  how come these words are fading
help me something is happening
  beyond my control I should
never
      have
            mentioned
                black
                      holes

Take Care in the Top End

Down by the billabong the bank is bare
this is the Top End and I'm taking care

the water so still and waterlily calm
so why do I feel a sense of alarm?

one small ripple from a log that's drifting
two small nostrils slowly shifting

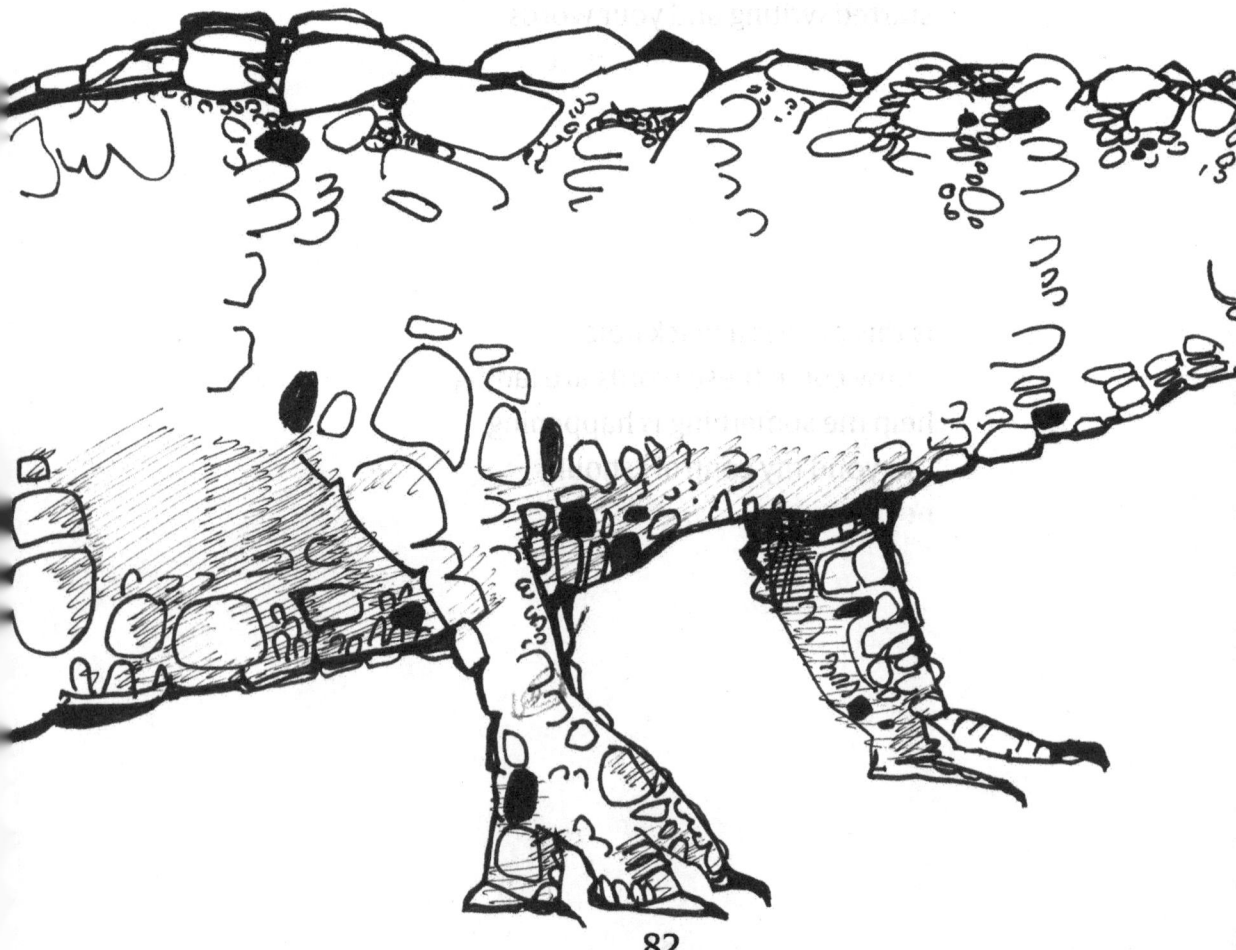

just a few metres in front of me
the teeth are glinting evilly

he lunges I jump it's a croc **heart stop**
it's a saltwater croc he lunges I jump
and I'm running like crazy towards a tree
but that croc's about to catch up with me

I take a running leap and grab on a branch
the croc's jaws snap like he's missed his lunch

   his eye doesn't blink
    and his breath really stinks

    hey croc, you got something better to do?
   no says the croc *I'm waiting for you.*

The Wave you've Waited For

you know it's the one – look at that green body of glass
wave-muscle, tons of it starting to foam at the lip
this one's gonna take you all the way, wait wait
NOW! launch, power up and you're on
surfing the face, kicking the turn
riding the beast, the best wave
and you're balanced to perfection
roaring in your ears
heaven is a hundred metres long

Yawn Alert

In every room
there's always a yawn
hiding in the corner

yawns are invisible
until they find a face
don't let it be yours

there's one
moving away from the wall
looking for someone to try itself on

don't change your expression
ignore that yawn

ignore ...
ignore ...

I'm being attacked by a monster yawn
aaaarrrhhhh

I've created a storm of yawns
STOP YAWNING

STOOOOPPP YAAAAWWWNING!

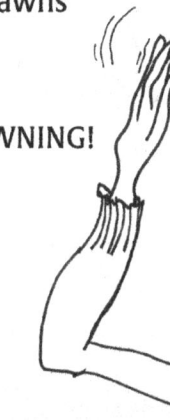

My Favourite Food

Broccoli cooked to sludge
brussels sprouts topped with fudge

squashed banana off the floor
gravy sticking to the door

slimy mushrooms three weeks old
ancient cheese growing mould

potatoes mashed with dirt and rocks
deep fried strips of dirty socks

tissues spread with vegemite
give me such an appetite

I'll eat anything you see
maybe I'll start eating me.

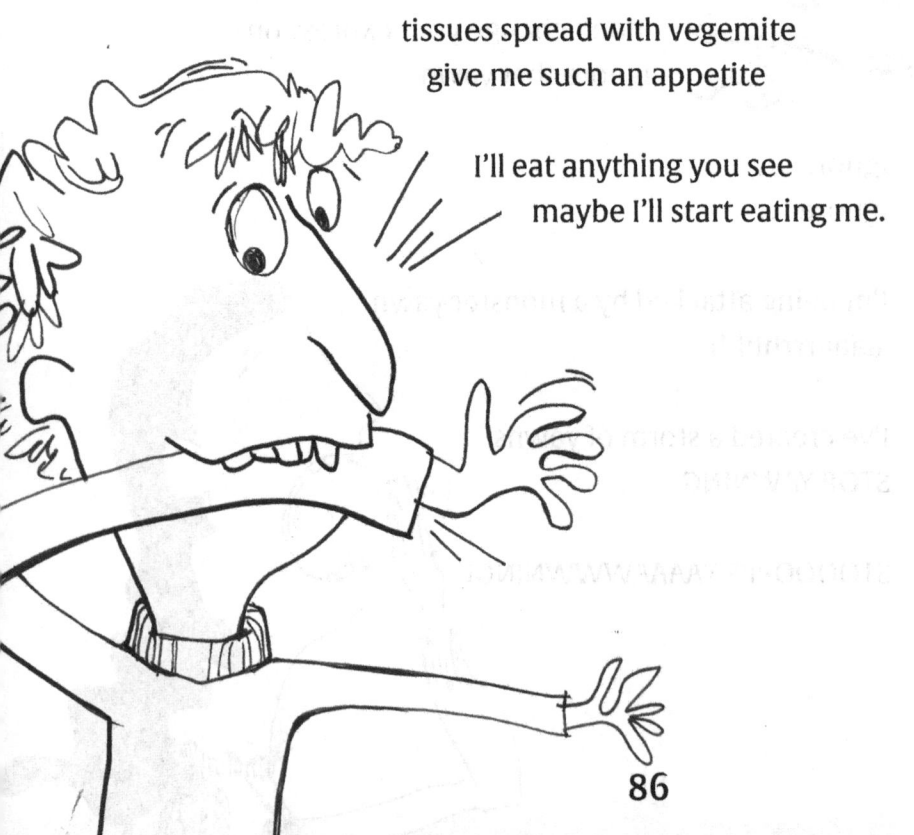

Wa, the Crow

aar aar
his name is wa
fast and sharp
he'll scratch your car

aar aar
travels far
smart and fast
colour of tar

aar aar
a crow called wa
got no time
for bla bla bla

aar aar
he travels far
aar aar
the crow called wa

I Wanna Be a Wombat

I wanna be a wombat
I wanna be a wombat
and waddle like a wombat
and here's the reason why

armour-plated bum fat!
intruder comes and I'm attacked
I swivel in ma tunnel shack
and crush them on the side

I wanna be a wombat
I wanna be a wombat
and waddle like a wombat
here's another reason why

biting on the bum fat
chasing other wombats
up and down the worn tracks
pulling off the big stacks
screeching like a tomcat

I wanna be a wombat
I wanna be a wombat
and waddle like a wombat
and here's another reason why

I'm a thirty kilo bomb-bat
I'm better than a bobcat
I waddle like a wombat
I wanna be a wombat
and that's the reason why.

Chair Rodeo

When you're a chair
people don't care
think you're just four legs
think you're just *there*

but people don't know
what chairs get up to
soon as people go
it's a big chair rodeo

chairs start tapping
rapping and bucking
chairs on two legs
all chairs rockin'

climbing out the windows
chairs cracking whips
chairs doing jumps
and nobody sits

so next time you
think chairs are dumb
you better get ready
to shift your bum.

The Strangest Pet

My strange pet is a house.
It's a hundred years old.

I love my pet house.
We go for long walks
of up to one millimetre.

When my house gets tired
I have to fetch the bulldozer.

But it's a very happy house
and friendly to other houses.

It eats dust, footprints
spilt juice and tradies.

There's only one problem
it's hard to cuddle a house.

Oh, and house-poo is HUGE.

The Adventures of a Foot

There was a battle
I survived
I am a foot
and I'm alive

I've taught myself
to hop along
my skin is tough
my spirit strong

all my toes
   have learnt to eat
      I'm looking out
         for other feet

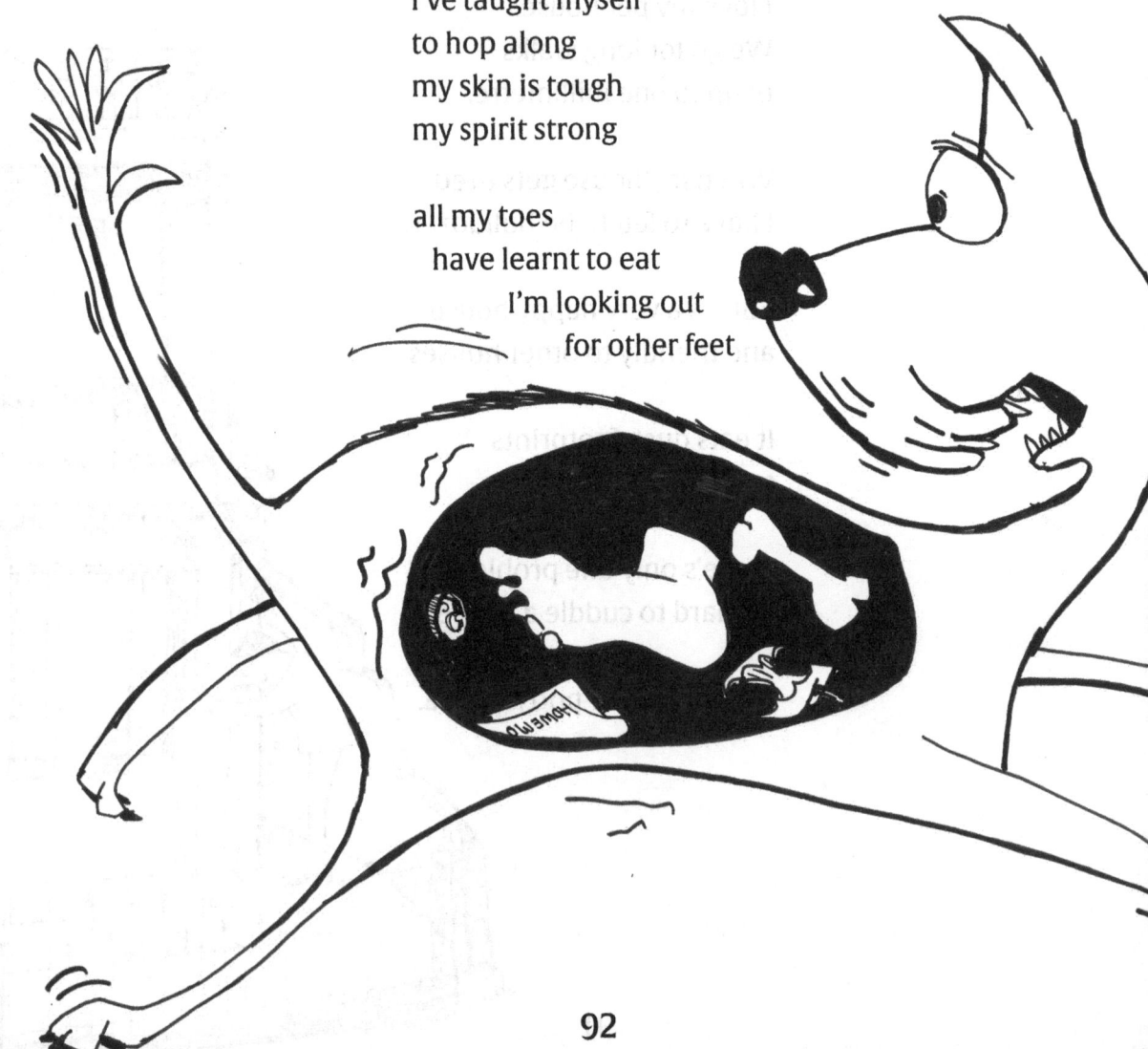

I don't like roads
I don't like cities
when cars hit feet
it isn't pretty

I met a dog
who swallowed me
I kicked and kicked
till I got free

as for people
they've no clue
they'd like to stuff me
down a shoe.

Nightmare of the Nose

There's a special kind of nightmare
when you're lying on your back
and you can't move a muscle
and everything is black

and your mouth is dry as paper
there's no feeling in your toes
and suddenly you realise . . .
you haven't got a nose!

A sniffing sound, you look around
light's coming from the floor
your nose is fluorescent green
and walking out the door

so you get up and you follow
your nose knows what to do
suddenly you're in the street
and your neighbour's noseless too

there are noses bouncing everywhere
on grass on cars in trees
the noise they make is horrible
like a tidal wave of sneeze

    STOP! you say but you can't shout
    you're frozen to the spot
    and the noses run towards you
    trailing fluorescent snot

AAARGH! finally you wake up
and the first thing that you do
is find the nearest mirror, check ...
YES! your nose is good as new.

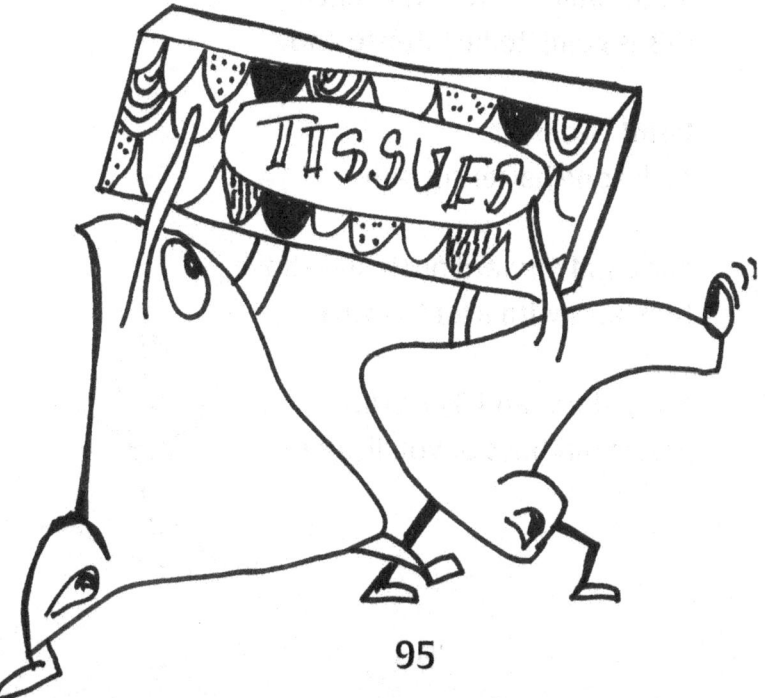

Big Black Bulls

Pawing dirt over his head
one Angus bull is seeing red

or could it be another bull?
Both of them are one-tonne fools

muscle-packed and extra large
yes, they are about to charge . . .

thundering at full speed gallop
drumming over dried-up paddock

Angus bull destroys the fence
this is going to be intense and

Bam! two bulls
make one battering ram

back and forward push and shove
two bulls with a lot to prove

body-slams and flying dirt
watch out boys or you'll get hurt

sure enough one bull is down
tongue hanging out and snorting foam

the other's limping, can't even run
and doesn't care because . . . **he's won!**

muuuuuuuuuuuuu

Storm at Night

Sounds like doom
    the distant boom
        fills your dream
            with scary scenes

staccato rattle
    it's a battle
        on the run
            from massive guns

cracks overhead
    you wake in bed
        night's turned to day
            a crazy play

bright-sky-flash
    of lightning gash
        flicker-splits
            two hundred hits

imagine if
    that million volts
        had found your head
            bang! You'd be dead!

Stingrays

Underwater the shadow
looks like a rock
then it moves closer
and you get a shock

big as a table
two metres wide
black-speckled silver
white underside

rippling past
it's a Stingray, it's huge
another close by
and they're hunting for food

circling for scraps
sweeping under the pier
trailing those barbs
but you've nothing to fear

Stingrays are curious
   gentle and calm
      leave them alone
         they'll do you no harm.

When You Feel Sad Sing This Song

Lyin' on ma bed
I'm feeling so sad
thinkin' about
the day that I had
people that pushed me
said I was no good
like I was nothing
from the wrong neighbourhood

and then my room
turns into a stage
the lights are dazzlin'
and it's time to rage
thousands of fans
are screaming for me
because I am a star
this is my destiny

U Rock

when you're sad
you feel bad
you're a sack, you're a drag
turn it up
turn it round
get your feet back on the ground
you're a star
you're the one
and you should be having fun
I'm telling you the good times
have only just begun
I'm telling you the good times
have only just begun.

About the author

Harry Laing is a poet and comic performer. *RapperBee* is his third book of poems for kids. His other books are *Shoctopus* (Bunda Press) and *MoonFish* (Ford Street). He's been teaching creative writing workshops in schools for over 20 years and still loves it. Harry lives near Braidwood on the Southern Tablelands of NSW where the wombats give him a hard time.

www.harrylaing.com.au

About the illustrator

Anne Ryan is an author, illustrator, artist and art educator living in Melbourne. Through school visits, artist in residence programs, workshops and Visual Arts specialist teaching, she has enjoyed sharing her creative processes and storytelling with young children for many years. Her love of picture books inspired Anne to participate as an illustrator on the Australian creators' stand at the Bologna Children's Book Fair in Italy 2017 and 2018. Her artwork was selected for the Illustrators' Wall at the Bologna Children's Book Fair 2021.